Bartle Frere

Christianity Suited to All Forms of Civilization

a lecture delivered in connection with the Christian Evidence Society, July

9th, 1872

Bartle Frere

Christianity Suited to All Forms of Civilization
a lecture delivered in connection with the Christian Evidence Society, July 9th, 1872

ISBN/EAN: 9783337347970

Printed in Europe, USA, Canada, Australia, Japan

Cover: Foto ©Andreas Hilbeck / pixelio.de

More available books at **www.hansebooks.com**

Christianity suited to all Forms of Civilization.

A Lecture,

DELIVERED IN CONNECTION WITH

THE CHRISTIAN EVIDENCE SOCIETY,

JULY 9TH, 1872.

BY

SIR BARTLE FRERE, G.C.S.I., K.C.B., D.C.L.

LONDON:

HODDER AND STOUGHTON,

27, PATERNOSTER ROW.

———

MDCCCLXII.

CHRISTIANITY SUITED TO ALL FORMS OF CIVILIZATION.

I HAVE been requested by the managers of this series of lectures to state to you the results of observation and experience in other countries as to the adequacy of Christianity to meet the requirements of the varying forms of civilization.

It will be my object to tell you what is—what I have seen myself—rather than what I imagine ought to be. I wish to meet the theory which, in one shape or another, is not uncommonly propounded in this country, that Christianity is a Semitic variety of religion, suited to Syria and to a people of Jewish or Arab origin, but little adapted to men of other races and other climates. I wish to show you, as far as the brief limits of a lecture allow, that experience proves Christianity to be a religion perfectly adapted to mankind of the most various races, and in every stage of civilization, from the lowest to the highest.

We must first define the meaning we intend to attach to some of the words which we shall have to use. For instance, the word " Christianity " itself has a signification widely different as used by different Christians, and still more different as used by writers who can in no sense be classed as Christian writers. I shall speak of it in this lecture as the religion which is a rule of life to the majority of religious people in England calling themselves Christians. We may take the Apostles' Creed, as generally received and interpreted among us here in England, as the symbol of the belief whose adequacy to meet the requirements of all forms of civilization I hope to illustrate.

Further let us bear in mind, that however much we Christians may differ as to particular articles of doctrinal belief, or of discipline, we all regard our Christian religion as depending on a revelation of some kind— as being something told us from without, in contradistinction to the modern theory, "that people have their religion as part of their growth, and that a man is not more responsible for his religion, than he is for the colour of his hair, or the length of his arm ; that, in fact, it grows as a part of himself." This is a convenient doctrine as getting rid of all personal responsibility in matters of belief, and is rather commonly met with in these days among many classes of professed Christians. We have not time at present to discuss it, or to show how fundamentally it is opposed to the idea of *any* religion as a rule of life. I will only therefore remark that we cannot recognize this description

as applying to Christianity, which we regard as em-
bodying truths and rules of conduct revealed to the
intelligence of man from an external power—it may
be through the senses, it may be through the conscience or the intellect, it may be recorded in books
or handed down in traditions ; but in whatever form,
it is an *external* something, which is able powefully
to modify the very nature of man, and all functions of
his intellect and spirit, as well as his physical being.

As a further preliminary we must consider what we
require a religion to do ?

Let us leave out for a moment the consideration of
all that relates to the world to come. Nor let us for the
present even stop to discuss the question whether mankind might or might not be better off without any
religion at all. Much ingenuity has been expended on
proving such a position, just as it might be in proving
that mankind would be better off without salt, or bread,
or meat. But the general sense of mankind is all the
other way, and our present purpose is comparative.
Let us look on religion as one of the things which men
generally think they require to aid moral and social
laws in making men better and happier, more prosperous in life, and more able to promote the well-being
both of believers themselves and of all in contact with
and affected by them. To what extent is Christianity,
as compared with other religions, adapted in these
respects to the wants of mankind under various forms
of civilization? This is the question which we pro-

pose to discuss, not by *a priori* arguments, but by examples and experience.

I. Let us first consider the case of wild tribes, who are, as nearly as we can judge, in what is called a state of nature. We have whole families, and even races, in Europe in a condition very little removed from that of the wild beasts; but they are generally a degraded and neglected form of mankind who have lapsed from a better state of civilization, and are hardly such good subjects for illustrating our argument as the wild tribes of India, who, so far as historical records show, have been from very early ages in a state at least as barbarous as that in which we have found them of late years. What I am now about to tell you applies to nearly one-fifth of the people of India. Some of them are not much removed above the condition of the aboriginal tribes in Australia. In the Andaman Islands there are remnants of a Negrillo race, who, though far better formed and well developed physically and mentally than the Australian race, have quite as little of artificial civilization about them. In the jungles of Central and Southern India are to be found tribes whose habits seem to approach much more nearly to those of apes than of men. A few of them are said to be absolutely without clothing, and to live habitually in trees; others have no better substitute for clothing than bunches of leaves, while with all of them the use of clothing is limited to the slightest imaginable amount of covering. A little more civilized than these are the jungle tribes, Bhils and Katkurees, and other races who live mainly by the chase. The great body of the tribes on our eastern frontier, the Sontalls and Koles, and many of the clans of Goandwana in Central India, and the Koolies and Thakoors of the west, are one step higher in civilization. They have huts and fowls and cattle, and some of them, especially on the eastern frontier, have slaves : all have some rude cultivation on spots cleared by burning the jungle. Again, one step higher, are tribes known as the Pariah or outcast tribes of Western and Southern India, apparently the remnants of aboriginal tribes conquered by the earlier invaders of Hindostan, and reduced to the condition of serfs or helots. The term "outcasts" hardly describes their condition, because they have never formed any integral part of the purely Hindoo communities ; but they are "outsiders" in every sense of the word —forced to live outside the village walls—forbidden to touch or draw water from the wells of the Hindoo community; and though often—in the Maharatta Country always—occupying recognized positions in the village economy as settled cultivators and artizans, they are strictly confined to those services which, however necessary, are associated in all countries with a certain sense of pollution ; they are scavengers, skinners of dead animals, and the like.

The more settled tribes frequently approach very

nearly in civilization to the simpler classes of Hindoo agriculturists and artizans. But they have this in common with their wilder neighbours, that they are all more or less Fetish or devil-worshippers—a fact which distinguishes them broadly from the great body of genuine Hindoos. Altogether of these races I have been describing there are, according to the latest estimates, not fewer than forty millions of souls within the British Empire in India and Ceylon, a population almost as great as that of France or Germany.

Their physical qualities resemble those of savages in every part of the world. All are great observers ; they have that peculiar quickness of eye and ear, and of all physical senses, which characterizes wild men, and which you see in any civilized man who, like the backwoodsman or remote colonist, has lived much among the solitudes of nature. But it is not only their external senses of sight and hearing and smelling which are wonderfully quickened by the necessities of the life they lead. Any one who lives much among them will be often astonished at the minute accuracy of observation evinced by them when they come first among the distracting sights and sounds of civilization. In the English official's tent or cutcherry they may appear perfectly dazed and confounded, watching every novelty of the scene around them, and with difficulty made to understand the business which brought them there—though it may be a capital charge, perhaps, of robbery and murder ; and yet these same savages, when by themselves afterwards, will imitate with the most unmistakable fidelity—and with infinite humour—every peculiarity of voice and manner in the foreigners with whom for perhaps the first time in their lives they had been brought in contact.

Their only wisdom is that of experience in all matters of daily life ; they have, of course, no book-learning, no philosophical systems—nothing of what some of our modern philosophers would call the shams or trammels of civilization. Careless of human life, they suffer little from the physical evils attendant on civilization. Their diseases are generally such as are the consequences of deficient or unwholesome food, or of want, or of malaria. Such of them as have fixed habitations, when they begin to find the spot where they live becoming unhealthy—when their fowls or their children die, or their grown folk suffer from fever—generally conclude that some evil spirits have entered the village, which they forthwith abandon, and move to a spot a short distance off. Every evil in life is attributed to some demoniacal or malicious agency. Their priests are generally little more than witch-finders or exorcists of evil spirits. The marriage-tie is lax among the ruder tribes, but invariably becomes stronger as the tribes become more civilized. They are generally far more truthful than their civilized neighbours, sometimes apparently from innate honesty, at other times from simplicity; but few of them appear to have that abstract regard for truth which we associate with the highest form of civilization. They are all, as a rule, kind and indulgent to their children ; but the death of a child is not generally a matter which affects them more than the death of their young cattle, and when hard pressed for means of subsistence there is little trace among the men of that self-sacrifice for the sake of children which is so common in many more civilized communities. There is, as a general rule, little veneration for age, when the old people become burdensome through inability to provide for themselves. A few tribes are still clearly addicted to human sacrifices as the most potent form of propitiating the powers of evil ; and most tribes have traditions which indicate that such practices were formerly more common.

One universal feature of all savage life is that everything goes to the strongest. It is not easy to convey to civilized men any definite notion of all that this peculiarity implies; still less to show how prone we are to relapse into—

"The good old rule, the simple plan,
  That they should take who have the power,
  And they should keep who can "—

when the checks imposed by a civilized organization of society are removed.

I will endeavour to illustrate both the tendency and its results by an instance which was related to me by an old friend, and which struck me as

showing how this natural tendency comes out whenever there is a real struggle for existence. My
friend was a very intellectual, shrewd Scotchman,
who was cured of his youthful fancies in favour of
savage life by being shipwrecked half-a-century ago
in one of the great old East Indiamen upon the
island called Inaccessible, in the Southern Ocean.
It so happened that the whole of the crew—with the
exception of the captain—and all the passengers, including a large detachment of troops, and numbering
several hundred souls of various ages and professions,
got safely to the rocky shores of the island, where they
lived for some months, supported by the provisions
they saved from the ship, and by the vast quantities
of eggs of wild-fowl which were found on the rocky
ledges of the island. One of the most prominent
characters on board the ship previous to the shipwreck
had been the surgeon—a man of weak physical powers,
but of great and varied intellectual attainments, and
of most popular manners and charming disposition. He
had possessed during the voyage an unbounded influence over both officers and men—was invaluable to the
captain as a supporter of discipline, and to the chaplain
as aiding his moral teaching. He had induced all the
young men on board to prosecute their studies regularly
under his direction, and was a leading authority with
regard to all the amusements by which the monotony
of the voyage was relieved. He was, in fact, a type of
what high intelligence in a civilized community can

achieve in the way of legitimate and useful influence. For some days after the shipwreck his old power continued, and was always exercised for the public benefit ; but after a while the pressing necessity felt by every soul of the shipwrecked community was the provision of water, which had to be procured from distant scanty springs, and the collection of a sufficient supply of birds' eggs to satisfy the calls of hunger. They had got, in fact, down to that stage of civilization at which the satisfaction of the first wants of nature in the way of food was of pressing daily importance. From that moment all the authority of the man of intellect vanished. He had not the physical strength to carry water or climb for birds' eggs, and the boatswain's mate—an illiterate man, of great physical power and energy, with other qualities fitted to shine in savage life—took the lead and kept it ; exercising despotic sway over the whole community as long as they remained on the island.

Possibly some of us might say, "this is all perfectly natural and proper ; the result must be a process of natural selection by which the most powerful physical natures will take the lead, and the consequence a gradual improvement of the race." But Indian experience of savage life does not at all confirm this view. The savage races are invariably smaller, weaker, and worse developed than the civilized. Many of the half-civilized are fine men, because they retain their habits of eating animal food, and thrive better than those neighbouring civilized races whose diet is exclusively vegetable ; but in such cases their mode of living and kind of diet combines many of the advantages of both civilized and uncivilized life. The results of purely uncivilized existence, so far as I have seen them, are invariably a decreasing population, decreasing size and health, a general tendency to degenerate and to assimilate more nearly to the habits of beasts of the forest. I should doubt if mankind would ever become extinct in the jungles of India, because the smallest remnant of human intelligence gives them such an advantage over the other creatures of the forest, that the extinction of the race seems a very remote contingency. But a gradual dwindling of mind, body, and soul is universally apparent wherever civilization does not intervene to counteract the tendency.

Our experience of the races I have been describing does not agree with the theories of philosophers who maintain that the perfect condition of human nature is to be found among people who live a purely material life, thinking only of matter and its properties, and obeying with unquestioning fidelity all the instincts of their material nature. Such a life *is* led by the most uncivilized and savage of the tribes I have been describing. If the theories of modern materialist philosophers were true, it seems to me these tribes ought to swallow up civilization and all its shams; but practice and experience prove that civilization swallows up them and their materialistic mode of life, and unless they become civilized they are invariably extinguished when they come in contact with civilized communities —notnecessarily by war or violence, but by the certain operation of civilization.

This brings us to the question of their religion. What is it, and how is it modified by contact with Christianity ?

First, let us observe that not one of them, as far as I am aware, is destitute of some form of religion. As to what may be the case in other parts of the world I cannot tell, but as regards the wild tribes of India—and some of them are probably quite as wild as any in the world—I know of none who do not possess a religion of some kind. It is true, I have been told by some of them in so many words, that "gods are for English gentlemen, respectable Brahmans, and Muhammedans, and that the poor children of the jungle do not pretend to or venture to possess any such luxuries as the gods of the people around them." But in so speaking they thought only of the gods whose shrines they saw whenever they visited the haunts of civilized men; and I never could hear of any tribe, however wild, the members of which did not possess a religion of some kind—a belief in the existence of beings of super-human power, whose active agency modifies the conditions and objects of life of all mankind. The religion of all the various tribes and classes I am speaking of is more or less Fetish worship ; that is, they have some form of religion, which consists not always in the worship of evil, but in a practice of deprecatory sacrifice, and petition to malevolent beings with a view to avert evil results to the worshipper or his friends. It is also an invariable feature of Fetish worship that the worshipper is able, by influencing the powers of evil, to effect mischief to his enemies, as well as to obtain good for himself. Time does not admit of more than a brief reference to a few of the commonest forms of Indian Fetish worship. Among the jungle tribes, beasts of prey, and notably the tiger, a common symbol of the spirit of evil, " Wagia," (the tiger-god,) is wor- shipped by widely distant and unconnected commu- nities. Next in popularity and universal acceptance is the worship of such epidemic diseases as are known among savages. "Matajee," the goddess of small- pox, " Mahamurree," the great death, or cholera, take a prominent place whenever these scourges of savage as of civilized life make their appearance. The sac- rifice of a fowl, or even a goat, which is a suitable propitiation of the tiger-god, is rarely efficacious when the goddess of epidemic disease makes her appearance. A rude procession is then organized ; a figure dressed up in.female garments, and ornamented as well as the means of the community allow, is worshipped and propitiated with sacrifices, conveyed to the limits of the village, or tribe, and there handed over to a neighbouring community, to be carried on or left in the jungle, in the hope that the figure has conveyed with it the seeds of disease, which will thus be passed on to the place of her new residence. I have known this system very efficacious in propagating instead of allaying the disease, in consequence of the terror inspired in the untutored inhabitants of the jungle at finding within their boundary the hideous figure which had been deposited there by their neighbours. If the community which has expelled the figure continues to suffer from the disease, they have no remedy but to disperse and fly.

For such people, I have heard it said in this Hall, " you must have a Fetish of some sort, and a stock or a stone is a better help to devotion than a priest or his sermon." * Let us consider how far this assertion is true—how far it accords with the facts we know.

Let us suppose for a moment the possibility of such a thing as a " Christian Fetish." I am using the words of those from whose opinions I entirely differ,

---

* " Fetishism is a natural concomitant of this stage of our "mental development"(*i.e.*, a stage of crass, savage ignorance); "* * * The only religion possible at this stage is the religion of "sense. * * * Christianity * * has far less chance of success "here than a religion which is purely Fetishistic. * * * If sen- "suous accessories are at all requisite, stocks and stones, idols "and oracles, are far better helps to devotion than the pulpit or "the priest—the surplice or the sermon."—*Lecture of Jairam Row, in St. George's Hall, November 12th,* 1871.

simply for the sake of argument. I would ask any candid opponent who chooses to describe the objects of worship which we place before our poorer and more ignorant brethren as " Fetishes," whether he really thinks such " Fetishes " as are habitually placed before their hearers, as objects of worship, by St. Peter, St. Paul, St. John, or by the priests of our own Church, have anything in common with such Fetishes as form the objects worshipped by the people I have been describing ? All Christians agree at least in this, that the religion they profess is applicable alike to learned and unlearned men, to the untutored savage and to the civilized philosopher. Hence the Christian Fetish, if such a Fetish there can be, must be alike the Fetish of the poorest and most ignorant peasant or savage, and of Newton, Bacon, or Locke, of Wilberforce, Las Casas, or Henry Marten.

But can such a thing as a " Christian Fetish" exist? or be preached from any Christian pulpit ? As I understand a Fetish, it is a being of evil, worshipped with a view to deprecate its wrath, rather than to propitiate its justice or mercy. Such a worship is opposed to the very fundamental notions of Christianity. Whatever nicknames may be given to partial or distorted statements of our doctrines, this, at least, is certain—that nothing like Fetish worship is consistent with the plainest teaching of any single book of the New Testament. There is scarcely a discourse or a parable of our Lord, or an epistle of His apostles, which does not teach that God is a God of love and mercy, and inculcate love towards all mankind as the foundation of Christian morality. This is the very opposite of Fetish worship, and it is simple misuse of language to talk of a Fetish as a possible part of any real Christian teaching.

But how does Christianity fare when it is brought in contact with Fetishism pure and real, such as is the religion of the wild tribes we have been speaking of? Is it found inoperative? ill-adapted to and inefficacious with an uncivilized and uneducated people? unimpressive upon those whose whole life is a struggle for material existence? or is it found to be mischievous in its effects, and inferior, either in power to affect at all, or to affect for good, in comparison with Fetishism?

To all these questions Indian experience during the last half-century must answer in the negative. Christianity has now been preached to Fetish-worshipping tribes in every stage of civilization, from naked savages of the wildest forests to the semi-civilized Fetish worshippers who are mixed up with the settled inhabitants of the cultivated country; and the invariable result has been to show that Christianity has power to prevail against Fetish worship, and that the results of the acceptance of Christianity by the Fetish worshipper are invariably to raise him in the moral and social scale, and to make him a civilized being. I believe there is no part of

India in which the power of Christian preaching to attract the attention of Fetish worshippers, to win them from the worship of evil and impure deities to the pure religion of Christ, and to raise them in the scale of humanity, has not been thus abundantly manifested. Most prominently are these results visible amongst the Shanars and other devil-worshipping races of Southern India ; the Kols and Goands of Central India ; the Bhils and Koolies, Mhars, Mangs, and Chumars of Western and Central India. Of all these races it may be truly said that Christianity, as far as its effects have been tried, has proved its possession of the promises of this life as well as of the next. In some parts of the country, as in Tinnevelly and Chota Nagpore, the number of actual baptized converts may be reckoned by tens of thousands, and all exhibit a marked improvement in the habits of social life. They are, as a rule, more temperate and chaste, more cleanly, more honest, and more industrious than they were before conversion.

In other parts of India, as in the Deccan, though actual conversions have not been numerous, the effect upon the whole community of outcasts has been marked and general. Scattered as they are, a few in every village in the country, there is no part of the province which has not more or less felt the influence of Christian teaching, and the result is not only a general inclination to turn from the gods of terror and uncleanness to the God of love, purity, and truth, but a remarkable social change which may hereafter bear political fruit, of which time does not now permit me to speak more in detail.

It is worthy of remark that these results are not confined to Christianity as taught in India by any single Church or sect of Christians. I have seen them abundantly follow the teaching of missionaries of our own Church, and of the Churches of Rome and Scotland—both Free and Established, of various Nonconformist bodies, and, in the most remarkable degree, of missionaries from various Churches of Germany, Switzerland, and America. There is comparatively little difference in the power and extent of the result, except what is obviously due to the number and earnestness of Christian missionaries employed, to their more or less perfect organization, and to the period during which their efforts have been directed to the conversion of Fetish-worshipping races and communities. Nor can it be said that the most learned, the wisest, the most accomplished or best endowed of the missionaries are always the most successful. On the contrary, the most wonderful results are sometimes effected by simple and unlearned men. From all these things we are led to the conclusion that such efforts owe their success to something which all the preachers of Christianity hold in common—the great, simple doctrines of Christianity which all believe—the plain, broad precepts of Christian morality which all teach.

What, then, generally speaking, may be summed up as the results of Christian teaching when brought to bear on the low form of civilization exemplified in the classes of which I have been speaking? It is everywhere a rising in the social scale—a civilizing and humanizing influence, tending to make the believer in Christianity a better man and a better subject. I would ask whether the same evidence of the power and effect of Christianity is not to be found in all we read regarding other parts of Asia, of America, of Africa, and of Polynesia—aye, in all we see around us of the effects of simple, earnest Christian teaching on London Arab life?

I have endeavoured thus briefly to describe the effects of Christianity acting on the wild Fetish-worshipping tribes of India as their own religion. But we have also to consider its effects as acting on them externally—as the religion of those in contact with them as neighbours or rulers. How, as compared with other religions, does Christianity suit them, when it is the religion of their more civilized neighbours or conquerors?

Now in India we can in this aspect compare the action of Christianity with that of various forms of Brahmanism, of Buddhism, and of Muhammedanism. Neither of the former in theory make any call on their votaries to propagate their own faith. The devout Brahman and Buddhist are both separatists in theory—seeking perfection through works and aspirations, among which the conversion of the ignorant and the civilization of the brutal find no place. It is true that both religions are more apt to spread among neighbouring communities of a different creed than is generally supposed, especially when those communities happen to be inferior in the scale of civilization ; but the process is one rather of annexation and imitation than of assimilation or conversion ; and the result is never more than the production of very spurious forms of Hindooism or Buddhism, the professors of which are never, even after the lapse of generations, accepted as true brethren by the genuine Brahman or Buddhist. Texts might doubtless be quoted from the dogmas of either, which would favour the work of the missionary or civilizer ; but personal purification and salvation is the main object of both, and any effort to save the souls or bodies of the savage tribes of the forest from death or disease, whether temporal or spiritual, is attended with a risk of pollution which would prevent almost any zealous Brahman or Buddhist from making the attempt.

Nor is the practice of the professors of these religions much better than their theory—coercion, expulsion, and destruction are the only modes of dealing with savages which find much favour with Hindu statesmen. When effectually coerced, a certain degree of toleration may be extended to them, and they may be protected as useful hewers of wood and drawers of water ; but that they have any inherent rights as members of the great human family, or that any obligation rests on the Government to protect or improve them, is a doctrine which never could reach the Hindu administrator through the teaching of his own religion.

The same may be said of the Muhammedan— though his religion, like our own, is essentially one of propagandism. If the savage is willing to be converted, he may, as a member of the great family of Islam, rise in the scale of civilization ; but there is little hope for the unconverted savage from any Muhammedan ruler, save in the most abject and unconditional submission ; and if Muhammedan practice is sometimes better than its theory in treatment of subject races of another faith, it is often far worse. As a general rule, unpersecuting neglect is the utmost the heathen savage or Fetish worshipper can hope for from his Muhammedan lord.

Vigorous government, in any native state in India, before the overshadowing advent of the great Christian power, generally meant more or less severity towards the jungle tribes. I will give you one of many instances I could quote. In my early life in the Deccan of India, I was engaged one day in trying one of these wild men for some depredation on the property of his civilized neighbours, when a Brahman, who had been high in office under the former Maharatta Government, came in to draw his pension. After listening attentively to the trial, he fell into talk on the subject of how Government should deal with such classes, and expressed as the result of his own large experience that nothing but the most severe modes of coercive treatment were of any real avail. He illustrated his argument by an anecdote of one of the great Soubadars of the Maharatta Peishwa, with whom he had served, and in whose province tribes of wild Bhils had been numerous and troublesome. Coercion and bribery had been tried, with equally little effect in mitigating their depredations. At last the Soubadar got wearied, and having invited all the principal chiefs to a feast, under pretence of largely increasing their subsidies, he set upon and slew them, whilst most of them were helplessly intoxicated, and "then the country," my visitor said, "had rest." He related the details of the tragedy not only without any symptom of horror or reprobation, but much as we might speak of the destruction of a family of wolves or tigers ; with a strongly expressed opinion that this mode of—what it is now the fashion to call "stamping out"—was the only sensible way of dealing with such vermin.

This, as I have said, was not a solitary instance of the spirit in which Hindu administrators of the old school would have dealt and did deal with the wild tribes. The case is far different now ; and I have no doubt all my young Indian friends would indignantly repudiate any such doctrines of extermination. But I would ask them where they learnt the principles on which they would now act ? Was it from their own Shasters, or from the writings and teachings of Christian priests, economists, and moralists? And whence did these latter derive their principles, if not from the storehouse of the Christian Scriptures?

From the days when Warren Hastings encouraged Cleveland to civilize the wild tribes of Eastern Bengal, as so graphically described by Heber, down to our own time, the administration of India has,.as a rule, acted towards the less civilized of our subjects and neighbours on principles which the Christian religion alone inculcates, and the result has in every way justified the system, as not only the most humane, but the most efficacious from a political and social point of view. I know in fact of no other system which can pretend to have reclaimed and raised to the position of useful members of civilized society whole tribes and communities of wild and uncivilized men ; and the most successful measures adopted for this purpose have been distinctly founded on the precepts of Christianity ; sometimes adopted knowingly and avowedly—more frequently, perhaps, unwittingly borrowed—through the medium of that code of Christian chivalry, which however adversely affected, at times, by ambition or cupidity, has never wholly ceased to actuate those Englishmen who, for centuries past, have been most energetic in extending British domination to every region of the habitable earth.

If any one requires proof of the literal truth of what I have said, let him consult the works in which it is recorded how Captain Hall and Colonel Dixon civilized the Mairs of Mairwarra in Rajpotana, or how General John Jacob and his lieutenants reclaimed the wild tribes of Northern Sind. A remarkable instance will be found in the records of Bhil civilization, from the first efforts directed by Mr. Mountstewart Elphinstone and Sir John Malcolm, in which Sir James Outram, Colonels Ovans and French, Keatinge, Douglas Graham, and Morris took part ; and instances more or less striking might be quoted from every province in India. The agents in these and similar civilizing proceedings have been frequently, but not always, men of deep and earnest religious convictions. But even in the case of those who made least pretension to a consistent profession of Christianity, it may be fairly asked whence did the actors get the principles on which they acted ? Not from the precepts of Greek or Roman, of Brahman, Buddhist, or Muhammedan. Still less from the social or economical theories of modern materialists or positivists. The principles on which the wild tribes of India have been, and are being, civilized, are identical with those which guide the teachers of our ragged and Sunday schools for the poor neglected children of this great metropolis. They are Christian principles, and are, as far as I know, to be found formulated nowhere save in the Christian Scriptures, wherein they are laid down as imperative rules of action in our dealings with our weaker and less civilized fellow men.

28

II. But let us now briefly consider the case of a second great class consisting of civilized men, broadly distinguished from the semi-savages of whom we have hitherto been speaking—men in the stage of civilization which has been reached by the great mass of the populations which we see around us here in Europe. They are living in organized communities, as artizans, traders, agriculturalists, professional men, following all the callings known to modern civilization. How does Christianity affect them? How far is it suited to them?

We shall find it next to impossible to answer this question conclusively, if we confine our attention to Europe and America, because the great majority of our people are, and have been for ages, professed Christians. We may, indeed, compare the Europe of Augustus' time with the Europe of our own, and draw our own deductions as to the effect of Christianity on our civilization. But we shall hardly escape debatable ground, as to how much is due to Christianity, and how much to other causes; or as to whether we might not have been better or worse, had the prevailing religion of modern Europe been other than it is.

Here, again, India may help us. You have there a great civilized population, four times as numerous as that of Christian America, as numerous as all the populations of Europe, excluding Russia. They are quite as advanced in all the arts of social life—I may say they are more advanced—than were the populations of Europe in the time of our grandfathers, before the great French Revolution and the outburst of modern mechanical invention. They have practically had nothing to do with Christianity, till within the last half century. But every other religion in the world is there and has been long represented on the grandest scale—idolatries more varied than the popular superstitions of Greece or Rome; a full third of all the Muhammedans in the world, and every form of esoteric religion, philosophies, mysterious and secret creeds without end.

How does Christianity fare in the face of all these powers of the air? Is it forced to give way? Is it silent? inoperative? Is it powerless, or put to shame?

I speak simply as to matters of experience and observation, and not of opinion; just as a Roman prefect might have reported to Trajan or the Antonines; and I assure you that, whatever you may be told to the contrary, the teaching of Christianity among 160 millions of civilized, industrious Hindoos and Muhammedans in India is effecting changes, moral, social, and political, which for extent and rapidity of effect are far more extraordinary than anything you or your fathers have witnessed in modern Europe. Presented for the first time to most of the teeming Indian communities, within the memory of men yet alive,—preached by only a few scores of Europeans, who, with rare exceptions, had not previously been remarkable among their own people in Europe for intellectual power or cultivation, who had little of worldly power or sagacity, and none of the worldly motives which usually carry men onward to success, —Christianity has nevertheless, in the course of fifty years, made its way to every part of the vast mass of Indian civilized humanity, and is now an active, operative, aggressive power in every branch of social and political life on that continent.

Of the external action of Christianity, as the religion of the conquering race, I will say but little ; other races, who were not Christians, in other ages, could and did conquer and civilize ; and if a mere handful of Christianized Europeans have succeeded in subduing scores of potentates, and people counted by scores of millions, they have only done on a very large and successful scale, what Greeks and Romans, Phœnicians and Assyrians, Egyptians, Teutons, Arabs, and other non-Christian races, have done before them, in all time past.

But let me note, as very noteworthy in itself, and as bearing especially on our subject, the spirit and the motives in which the conquerors of our own nation and time have acted ; because they are very different from anything you will find in the spirit or motives of action of any non-Christian race of conquerors I ever heard of. We have had, it is true, in our Indian conquests, enough of ambition, lust of conquest, cupidity, and all the meaner motives which actuate mankind in aggressive wars on their neighbours ; but I would ask you what has been the general national sentiment in approving each successive acquisition ? I do not speak of the motives of individual actors, but of the English nation at large, in ratifying and retaining the conquests from time to time achieved.

I answer, without hesitation, that it has been a feeling of duty towards the conquered—a conviction that we could not recede without abdicating the power of doing good to great masses of mankind, and thus permitting the existence of much preventable evil. No lower motive would, I feel sure, have sufficed to make the English nation at large approve the action of her children in India in time past, or would now induce Englishmen at large to continue to sustain the burdens and responsibilities of such a charge. It may be a mistaken view—that is matter of argument ; but it exists —that is matter of fact, and it is distinctly traceable to the system of morality founded on Christianity— the duty of doing good to your neighbour—which the nation at large recognizes as its rule of action, and it has a very important bearing on the value of Christianity as a civilizing agent. You will find nothing of the kind in the motives, as far as we know them, of any non-Christian nation. But it is singular that you do find them most distinctly marked among the most potent moving causes which have impelled other Christian nations to the conquest of non-Christians. I do not speak now of crusaders, or of the religious element which was traceable among the motives of the Spanish and Portuguese conquerors of past ages, though you know how potent and how elevating, as far as it went, that element was ; and how, as the religious motive became fainter, all that gave force as well as dignity to the action of the conquering nation seemed to disappear ;—but I would ask you to note how largely the desire to use power for the good of subject races actuates another nation which is perhaps even more than ourselves a conquering power in Asia.

We hear continually of the ambition and rapacity of Russia ; but we are apt to forget that there is a power urging Russia on to subjugate and civilize her barbarous neighbours, which is more potent and more persistent than worldly ambition or cupidity, and that is, the religious duty of Christianizing and civilizing : any one who, in estimating the forces of Russian aggressive movement, left out of view the impulse derived from religious convictions among the leaders of national thought—that it was a national religious duty to extend to all barbarians around them the blessings of being within the pale of the Russian Church—would leave out of calculation the most energetic element of the motive power.

This notion of doing good to the conquered is, moreover, an element not traceable among the motives of Assyrians, Romans, Saracens, or other conquering non-Christian nations.

C

We are not now arguing an abstract question of right or wrong. The desire of conquest is probably one of the most powerful and universal of human instincts. What we are now considering is how this universal instinct is modified by peculiarities of religion ; and what I wish you to note is, that in the case of our own nation and of the Russian—two of the great conquering Christian nations of modern days —considerations of which we can distinctly trace the origin to Christian morality add greatly to the effective force of the natural instinct, whilst they elevate and humanize it in a manner of which no trace is to be found in the action of the great conquering nations of other ages and creeds.

We have spoken hitherto of the external action of Christianity on non-Christian communities, such as we find in India. But what are its internal effects when it is received as their religion by the members of those communities who are at about the same level of general civilization as the mass of Europeans in the middle of the last century ? Does Christianity act at all on them ? and how ?

Let us look first at their social life—and here alone the subject is so vast, that one can, in the compass of such a lecture as this, barely touch on one or two characteristic points. Let us, for instance, consider the action of Christian teaching on Indian caste.

I need hardly remind you that all Indian civilized communities have one general characteristic which distinguishes them from similar communities in other parts of the world and in other ages—they are all bound by the traditions and practices of Hindoo caste. Volumes would not suffice to describe Hindoo caste and its effects, social, religious, and political. But there is an aspect in which it may be presented which may give you some faint idea of its nature and power, though it represents only one of the peculiarities of the great caste system. The peculiarity to which I allude is that it is a great system of trades' unions, more universal and better organized than any of the unions with which we are acquainted in Europe. Their origin in India is lost in antiquity. The earliest histories we possess recognize the system as one which had already grown up, and it appears more or less to have swallowed up and assimilated the foreign elements and nationalities which at different times have been imported into India. As far as experience goes, Christianity alone appears to have the power of resisting the absorbing influences of Hindoo caste.

It must not be supposed that the results of caste are altogether evil. How much mischief caste does I have not time to describe, but I will briefly refer to some of its good effects. It maintains a high standard of skill in all the arts of life. Even in a country which for the great part of a century has been the theatre of incessant desolating war, artizans, and even artists of the highest skill, are still to be found, owing their existence, or the possession of their arts, mainly

35

to the system of caste, which binds every man to the profession of his forefathers. More than this : caste has a great immediate effect in maintaining a moral standard. I do not say that in the long run, and in remoter results, the institution of caste is not one of very immoral tendency. It is, I believe, infinitely inferior in point of morality to the system of Christian morals ; but speaking with regard to immediate results, there can be no doubt that one of the primary effects of a strict system of caste is to maintain a very considerable strictness of morals.

Of its evils I will only select two. It prevents anything like national union, and it ensures a more or less rigid form of social slavery.

It is, I need hardly tell you, diametrically opposed to all the principles of Christianity. A religion which teaches, as fundamental doctrines, the essential unity of the human race—the brotherhood of every member of that race—and the potential possession by every such member of every blessing of this world, and of a boundless future ;—such a religion can have nothing in common with a great system whose essence is divisions innumerable, impassable here and hereafter, and practically annihilating the brotherhood of man. Christianity is, as you all know, perfectly compatible with a strict observance of gradations in social life, but of anything approaching the Hindoo system of caste it is the declared enemy. What then, as matter of experience, is its effect on the great mass of the civilized Hindoo communities, which are, with such rare exceptions, devoted adherents of caste ?

I answer shortly that intimate contact with Christianized Europe and a general diffusion of some slight knowledge of Christianity have been the death-knell of caste as the social bond of Hindoos. Such a system— the growth of thousands of years, among hundreds of millions of people—does not die in a day. It may be that only the first blow has been struck, but that blow has been a fatal one. It may take ages to work out the result, but the result can no longer be doubtful. It is not I alone who think so. You cannot gain the confidence of any thoughtful, honest, educated Hindoo, without finding out that this is his conviction. He may put many subsidiary causes in the foreground. Our superior military strength, and our freedom of political and social thought and action—our railways and other means of rapid intercommunication—our free press—our all-embracing literature and open education—our uniform laws,—these and many other agencies will occur to him as the most efficient solvents of his ancient social system. But he instinctively feels, what we ourselves are sometimes slow to perceive, that all these institutions and agencies are somehow the products and offshoots of our religion—that Christianity is logically and legitimately the foundation, the wellspring of influences, under a hundred shapes, moral and material, which, while they constitute our national life and strength, are destructive of things as they have hitherto been in Hindoo social life. He feels that the system of caste is doomed, and can never more reign, as it reigned but one generation ago, over the millions of Hindostan. Moreover, most thoughtful Hindoos are ready to confess that caste would have little chance of a reprieve even if we were turned out of India to-morrow. The strange truths which sink so deep into the hearts of people, and influence all their thoughts and actions, have not been taught by any State agency, and form no part of the apparatus which the English rulers have consciously employed. Indeed, it is apt to be charged as a reproach against our Government, that it has been too indifferent to missionary work,—and the charge is well founded, as far as general abstinence from all active co-operation can make it ; but I believe such abstinence to have been necessary and right, and in the result conducive to the spread of Christianity. Experience shows that a temporary withdrawal of the protection of the English Government, such as occurred in some parts during the Mutiny years of 1857-8, so far from extinguishing Christianity, helps to spread it ; and candid and thoughtful Hindoos are not slow to perceive that even if the English were now to leave India and were not succeeded by any other Christian power, it would still be impossible to counteract the destructive influences already at work, and that caste, as a system of impassable social divisions, must, ultimately, give way before the ideas which have taken root during a few generations of close contact with Christian Europe.

It would be impossible to contemplate without a shudder such results as the solution of all the ancient bonds of society, among so many myriads of people, were it not that the new influences have shown themselves at least as potent in binding mankind into new social combinations as in dissolving old social ties.

It is a curious fact that Christianity—whilst, as one of its fundamental principles, abjuring all claim to interfere authoritatively in matters of social or political organization, whilst inculcating the paramount duty of acquiescence and obedience to all lawful social arrangements and political institutions—has proved capable, beyond all other systems, of inspiring successful attempts at political and at social organization. Since the Roman society and polity began to decay, men enthusiastically imbued with the spirit of Christianity have ever been foremost in the task of building up that great fabric of European civilization which now dominates over the world. Whether in the wilds of Scandinavia, or among idolatrous Teuton hordes, in the cloister, in the camp, in the parliament, or in the guild of mediæval Europe—or, in later ages, asserting by speech, by pen, or by sword, the rights and obligations of mankind—the strongest and most successful organizers and constructors, social as well as political, have ever been

men of the strongest, deepest, most earnest religious
Christian convictions; differing, it may be, most
widely as to particular doctrines of their common faith
or particular practical applications of their theories,
but all deriving their inspiration from one common
source, and referring, as the ultimate authority for all
they do, to one book, briefer than the scriptures of any
other faith, and which inculcates all its moral precepts
with a clearness and simplicity which an intelligent
child can comprehend as perfectly as the most
advanced philosopher.

We may learn something of the comparative power
of Christianity, as a civilizing and constructive agency,
by comparing the great ecclesiastics who advised
Charlemagne, and Alfred, the Conqueror, Edward the
First, and our Tudor sovereigns, or the religious men
who in later days have worked out our present political system, with the Roman philosopher, the Hindoo
recluse, or the Muhammedan fakeer, to whom the
conquerors of other nations might have had recourse
for advice in organizing their dominions. We shall
do well to remember that the great organizers of our
own nation were generally typical examples of
the Christianity of their own day; when they were
assured that mankind needed the devotion of their
lives and labours, the argument was all-powerful to
draw them to the service of the State. Is there any
other religious system which thus makes public duty
a religious obligation? I cannot find it in Greek

or Roman philosophy, absorbed in the search for truth; still less in the Hindoo or Muhammedan systems, where the highest merit is attributed to ascetic observances which are utterly incompatible with attention to worldly affairs.

I mentioned as two prominent evils of the Hindoo system of caste, that it prevents anything like national union, and reduces the bulk of mankind to social slavery.

How effectual a cure Christianity supplies to the latter tendency needs no argument or illustration from me; but a word on its civilizing effect as a bond of national union. I can speak from experience, that the want of such a bond is most keenly felt by educated natives of India, of every class and creed, who desire to see their own countrymen rising in the scale of civilized nations. It is possible that at one time, under native sovereigns, caste, after a fashion, supplied such a bond. Its iron rules bound together all ranks and classes, and the political edifice was stable as long as all external influences were excluded; but all depended on the strictness of such exclusion, and it is possible, that even without the foreign invasion to which Hindoo caste owes its destruction, the edifice must in time have been sapped by influences which, like Christianity, do not necessarily require foreign agency for their introduction. However that may be, many educated Indians are convinced that the bond of caste can no longer be relied on; and even those who have no leaning to Christianity feel that whatever else may be proposed in the shape of new philosophies or systems of education, all lack the essential element of including the lowest as well as the highest classes in its grasp. Caste did this by including all in one bondage—Christianity does it by embracing all in one brotherhood. What else can be relied on, in these days of vast nationalities, which render feudal subordination so impotent, I know not.

For the present, patriotic Indians are generally content to acquiesce in foreign dominion, as the sole alternative to internecine civil discord. The time, I believe, must come when they will see that the influences which form the real bond of union between their foreign rulers are equally capable of uniting the scattered elements of their own social and national existence, and they will accept Christianity as that civilizing element which alone can render their own independent national existence possible.

But the time when this truth can obtain general acceptance is probably still distant, and educated Indians generally hold that some reform of their own system is still possible, and far superior to anything which Christianity can offer them. Their arguments are naturally powerful with those who are living entirely for the present—for the enjoyment of the things of this world, and who have no object but to make the most of this present life. For all such it must be confessed that the attractions of Christianity are less marked, when it is compared with any great worldly system, which, like the Hindooism or Muhammedanism of the trading, mercantile, and agricultural classes, places its *summum bonum* in a well regulated enjoyment of the things of this life. The lofty aims and self-denying precepts of Christianity have comparatively small attractions to those who are devoted to the pleasures of sense, to the accumulation of wealth, or even to many forms of intellectual luxury. For all such, the worship of Aphrodite or Mammon, whether in an abstract form, or in the form so commonly seen in India—the actual material worship of the creature—presents superior attractions. It is when the world and the things of the world, its pleasures and ambitions, cease to be the first objects of desire, that Christianity offers, to those who have been absorbed in the pursuits of the world, that which is not to be found in any other religion. To the prosperous trader, artizan, or agriculturalist, thriving in his own business, and wishing only to enjoy the good things it obtains for him, almost any religion, or no religion except the worship of himself, may suffice. He cannot be capable of the happiness which a Christian philanthropist, or a devoted Christian, can attain even in this life; but he can at least enjoy things as they are, and, if he can keep out of sight the future, and his obligations to those around him, he may live in great enjoyment. But it is otherwise when suffering or adversity overtake him, when he becomes anxious regarding the world beyond the grave, or seeks to know his duty to his fellow-men. In all these respects there is no comparison between the teachings of Christianity and those of any other form of religion. In adversity or in suffering, or when the conscience is aroused to ask what is our duty with regard to our fellow-men—no religion can give a perfectly satisfactory answer except Christianity; and the results of experience in India do not in any respect contradict what we should *a priori* expect in this respect. Missionaries tell us that they make small way among the prosperous traders or farmers, except when griet has softened the heart, or adversity has shown a necessity of some support other than that which can be derived from worldly enjoyments.

III. But we have still to consider the action of Christianity as a civilizing element on a third class of men,—infinitely smaller in number than either of the great classes we have been considering,—but most important as directors of the opinions of the world. I allude, of course, to those who are raised above the sordid material wants of the first class we have described, whose main object is not, like the great majority of the second class, how to exist, or enjoy life, but rather to teach mankind the end and objects of life and the best mode of living. These are the educated few who are the great teachers of mankind. How does Christianity affect or act on them?

I might dwell on habits of mind which are most congenial to Christianity, and which are distinctly fostered by it, and which are also peculiarly characteristic of some of the greatest teachers of mankind ; such are love of truth, and teachableness of disposition. It might, however, be truly said that such habits of mind are not peculiar to Christianity, and that they are to be found in the greatest teachers of all ages and creeds.

It is difficult in Europe to imagine what would be the condition of things apart from that Christianity in the midst of which every member of every class has been brought up, and which must unconsciously, by its influence or traditions, have more or less modified every opinion he holds.

But in India we have, in their unaltered original form, the prototypes of every system of philosophy which has ever existed in Europe, and we may learn something of the relations between those systems and Christianity, as a civilizing element, by observing the attitude of Oriental teachers of philosophy in all its branches towards our religion when it is presented to them.

Time, of course, does not admit of even the barest enumeration of the various schools of philosophy, still less of an examination of their tenets. But there are a few broad characteristics of the grander divisions of Oriental teaching which it may be well to notice, however briefly, with reference to their general bearing on civilization.

There is this common to them all—their philosophies are all for philosophers. They aim to teach the
teachers of mankind, and so indirectly act on mankind
at large ; but the notion of a teaching which, like that
of our Lord and · His apostles, was to be received,
wholly and completely, by all the body of disciples,
and which, as far as it is necessary to happiness in this
world or the next, was to be learned as perfectly by
the poor and needy as by the rich—this notion, which
pervades all Christianity, is utterly opposed to all
Oriental philosophies. It is to be found more or less
perfectly expressed, and not unfrequently obviously
borrowed from Christianity, in several of the eclectic
religions, which, from time to time, spring up in the
east, and have, from this cause mainly, acquired great,
and often permanent, popularity ; Sikhism and its
derivatives, like the Kuka schism, owe much of their
popular acceptance to this feature in their teaching; so
do the precepts of Kubeer Punt, and of Tukaram, the
popular Maharatta poet ; but to the higher Oriental
philosophies it is unknown, and its absence gives to
Christianity, which possesses it in the fullest degree, an
immense practical advantage over them, as a civilizing
element.

Something of the kind may be found in the brief
formula of the Muhammedan Creed, the repetition of
which constitutes almost the sole intellectual passport
for admission to Islam ; but the whole genius of the
philosophies which have received any bias from

Muhammedanism is exclusion of the vulgar. Poverty is inculcated as almost necessary to a high tone of sanctity, but the ruling idea is the exaltation of self— the exact opposite to that denial of self, which is the first step in Christian practice, and which makes Christianity essentially a religion for all mankind, and not for any one sect or nation.

This is the most important element in what, for want of a better word, I would term the "aggressiveness" of Christianity. The earnest Christian is irresistibly impelled by the spirit of his religion to communicate its benefits to others. He may not rest whilst any remain in misery or darkness. This aggressive spirit is of wonderful power as a civilizing agency. There is nothing like it in the spirit of Brahmanism or of Buddhism; and the aggressiveness of Muhammedanism is as infinitely inferior, in power and in endurance, as fear is inferior to love, as a motive of human action.

And this suggests a word on Christian toleration, which seems to me an equally distinctive feature of Christianity, and a most potent element of civilizing energy. There is nothing of it in pure Muhammedanism. It is not to be found in the Koran, with its more than Mosaic exclusiveness, and its energy in exterminating all difference of opinion. Great civilizing Muhammedan sovereigns like Akbar were compelled to import from Christianity, or its derivatives, that toleration which was their glory, and the secret of their success as benefactors of mankind. It seems to me that it is the

47

absence of this element which causes the sterility of Muhammedanism, and its want of power as a civilizing agency ; and as this feature is the essence of Muhammedanism, we cannot hope for anything of a real permanent civilizing influence from any modifition of that creed.

This is of more importance to us here in Europe than we might at first suppose, because, if there can be such a thing as Muhammedanism without a genuine faith in Muhammed, we have amongst us very popular creeds which have strong affinities to that religion. Next to self-worship, which is common in many other creeds, the most striking and usual aberration of Muhammedanism is towards the worship of the God of forces, or of success ; towards a belief that all the enjoyments of sense are the rightful heritage of the faithful who dare to seize them, and towards uncompromising and unarguing hostility to all who differ from the true believer's creed. The same spirit is manifest in all these respects in many of the anti-Christian schools of modern European philosophy and literature. Many grave treatises, and many more romances, of the present generation among ourselves have more of the inspiration of the Koran than of the New Testament, and if the rules and proceedings of the Fenian organization or the Parisian Commune were studied without a knowledge of the time and place where they were enacted, they would be more likely to be attributed to the camps of Omar or

Tamerlane than to the heart of Christian society in this century.

But to turn to the spirit of toleration to be found in other creeds. The toleration of the Brahman or Buddhist philosopher, striking as it appears at first sight, proves when examined to be simple indifference or neglect.

The absence of all active spirit of persecution, as long as the opponent is quiescent and submissive, which makes both Brahman and Buddhist practically so tolerant, is the offspring of contempt, and has nothing in common with the toleration which springs from the desire to do by all men as we would that they should do by us.

Time is wanting for any detailed comparison of the civilizing tendencies of either class of creeds with those of Christianity. I will mention but one obvious tendency of the teaching of each, which seems to me to place it, as compared with Christianity, in a position of decided inferiority.

Of the innumerable schools of Brahmanism, none is more popular in India than that of materialists, who teach that we can know nothing, certainly, save of matter and its properties; and that belief in what we call life or spirit, save as functions and properties of matter, —and by consequence any belief in a spiritual deity, —is a hopeless error and delusion. Something of the same kind is sometimes taught among ourselves, and into its truth or falsehood we will not now enter. But of its value as a civilizing agency we may form some idea, if we consider that there is hardly one of the practices which the English Government has been engaged in putting down, in the interests as we believed of all humanity and civilization, which is not clearly defensible under any moral code which can be deduced from such a creed.

For instance, infanticide, or at least the slaying of all children for whose nurture ample provision cannot be assured, is clearly defensible upon materialistic principles. So is the practice of Suttee, and the slaughter of all who have an incurable disease, or who from age or infirmity are unable to provide for their own subsistence. The great community of Thugs have excellent materialistic reasons for their mode of possessing themselves of the property of others, nor do I see how any form of rapine or appropriation, which practically enunciates the right of the strongest, can be objected to by any strict materialistic philosopher. Clearly there is no form of vice, so long as it is not directly prejudicial to health, from which a thorough-going materialist need be restrained. He is himself the sole judge of right or wrong, nor need he regard anything except in its relation to his own physical enjoyment.

Pressed with considerations of this kind, the Brahman materialist generally evades all obligation to construct any theory of moral duty. The only obligation he acknowledges is to find out the true nature and laws of matter, and how he can best live in accordance with those laws. The search is a long one, and while it is in progress the whole world may go on its way—unenlightened, unless it will follow the researches of the philosopher.

Surely there is nothing in such systems which can compare to the work, past or possible, of Christianity as a civilizing agency.

Nor is the case much better if we turn to Buddhism, the worship of pure reason, of which also one could find examples under other names among ourselves. No doubt it has achieved, in times past, triumphs of civilization of which there is scarcely any parallel in history. But it is equally clear that there is some defect which causes it now to give way, as a practical civilizing element, before Christianity. As a religion for all mankind (apart of course from all question of its truth) Buddhism is proved, by the inexorable logic of facts, to be weaker than Christianity.

It seems to me, the cause is not far to seek— Buddhism places its *summum bonum* in escape from passion, and from all connection with matter, from life and from existence, as involving passion. Such a system may evolve a high morality, or construct a great fabric of political wisdom; but it has nothing to offer mankind, nothing which comes so home to the instincts of all humanity as the Christian doctrines of the resurrection of the body and life everlasting in union with a glorified body. We may debate for ever over the proof of either doctrine; but as matter of fact and experience, there can be no doubt that they appeal to the hearts and instincts of mankind in a manner which the atheistic annihilation taught by the Buddhist philosopher never can.

Something of the feeling which I have endeavoured to express, of the paramount power of Christianity as a civilizing agency, and a bond of political union, is apt to show itself instinctively where it might least be suspected.

If a despot in Christendom is anxious for his throne, or if politicians find that the people long neglected are getting loose from all social and political ties, they are apt to call in the Christian teacher, as though he possessed some spell, the utterance of which could calm the wild passions of unrestrained and untaught humanity. Such men forget that Christianity is no charm or magical device, and that its power rests in the hearts of believers. Let them be wise in time, and before they put away from them the teachings of Christianity, and deliberately abjure its obligations as their rule of political and social life, let them remember that such gifts are not often twice offered to men or nations; and that to nations, as to men, it may happen, after once rejecting them, to find no place for repentance, "though they seek it carefully with tears."

www.ingramcontent.com/pod-product-compliance
Lightning Source LLC
Chambersburg PA
CBHW021234260626
47172CB00002B/762